ERIS TO THE RESCUE

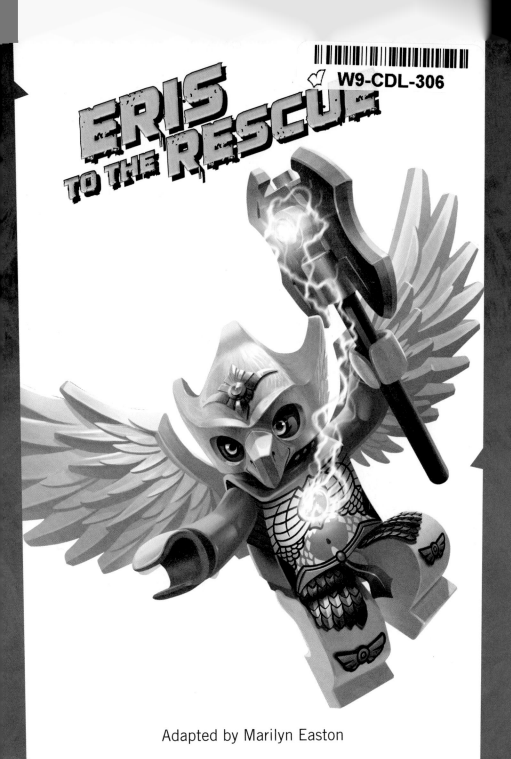

Adapted by Marilyn Easton

SCHOLASTIC INC.

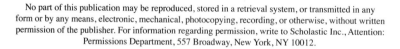

ISBN 978-0-545-56671-1

LEGO, the LEGO logo, the Brick and Knob configurations, the Minifigure and LEGENDS OF CHIMA are trademarks of the LEGO Group. ©2013 The LEGO Group. Produced by Scholastic Inc. under license from the LEGO Group.
Published by Scholastic Inc. SCHOLASTIC and associated logos are trademarks and/or registered trademarks of Scholastic Inc.

12 11 10 9 8 7 6 5 4 3 2 1   13 14 15 16 17 18/0

Printed in the U.S.A.   40
First printing, September 2013

MIX
Paper from
responsible sources
FSC™ C020056

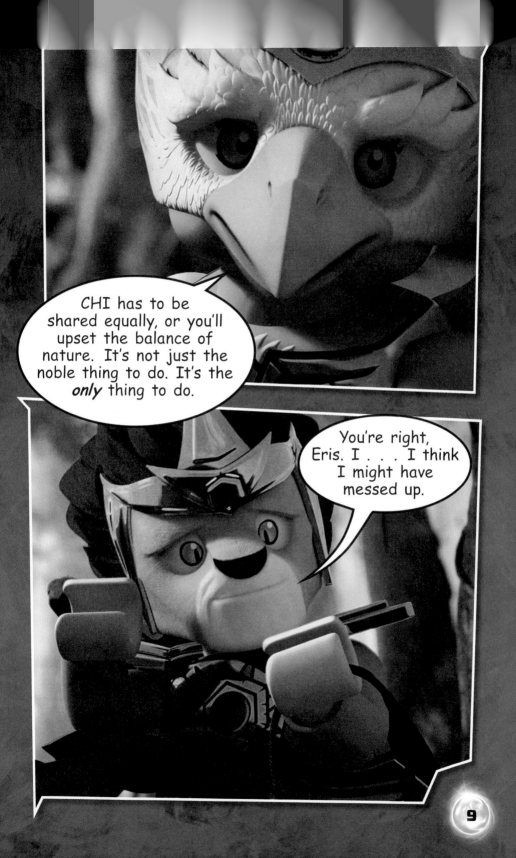

CHI has to be shared equally, or you'll upset the balance of nature. It's not just the noble thing to do. It's the *only* thing to do.

You're right, Eris. I . . . I think I might have messed up.

Uh, Master Cragger, Laval is outside. He says he wants to give us some CHI.

What?! But he'll ruin my big plan!

Don't worry, Brother.

This can work to our advantage.

Cragger meets Laval outside.

Look, I might have made a tiny mistake when I took your CHI. Sorry.

Gna! You'll *really* be sorry if you give me that CHI. I will use every last orb to destroy you, your father—

—and your entire tribe!

That's it. You're never getting our CHI!
Crocodile Troops! Did you hear him? We're never getting *their* CHI. So let's get him!
Uh-oh . . .

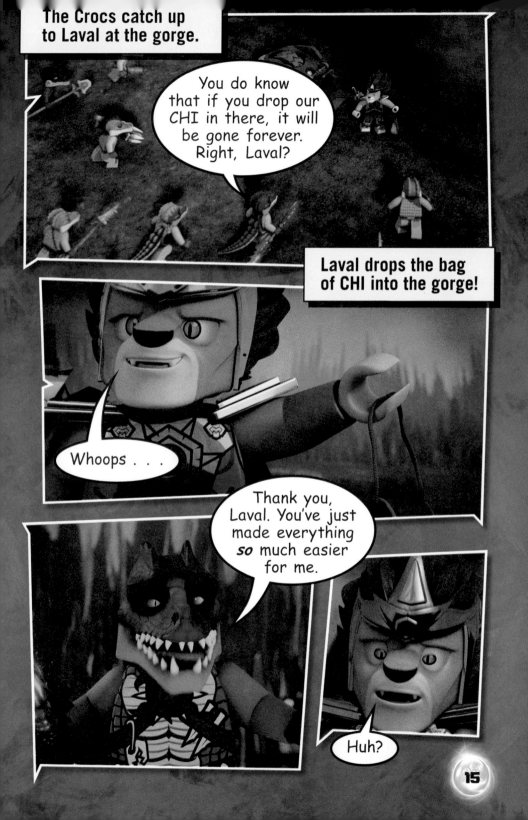

The Crocs fire pulse blasters at the plane.

We've got you now!

BOOM!

Eris and Laval crash-land across the gorge.

That was close. We're safe, for now.

Laval searches for the Legend Beast. Time is running out!

Legend Beast, where are you?

We need your help!

The Croc Troops catch up to Laval!

I guess your Legend Beast doesn't want to save you.

Cragger reveals he has a CHI Orb, too . . .

Did you think you stole all our CHI?

AARRGH!

. . . and CHIs up!

Oh, you and your silly fights. Don't you know there's no *winning* without a *winning smile*?

RRAARRGGHHH!

Plovar makes a quick escape!

Does this mean you want to reschedule?

Laval rallies a cheer from his friends.

We have beaten back the enemy again!

For Chima!